George Grenville

The Speech of a Right Honourable Gentleman

On the motion for expelling Mr. Wilkes, Friday, February 3, 1769. Fourth

Edition

George Grenville

The Speech of a Right Honourable Gentleman
On the motion for expelling Mr. Wilkes, Friday, February 3, 1769. Fourth Edition

ISBN/EAN: 9783337195748

Printed in Europe, USA, Canada, Australia, Japan

Cover: Foto ©Andreas Hilbeck / pixelio.de

More available books at **www.hansebooks.com**

THE
SPEECH

OF A

RIGHT HONOURABLE

GENTLEMAN,

ON THE

MOTION

FOR

Expelling Mr. WILKES,

FRIDAY, FEBRUARY 3, 1769.

THE FOURTH EDITION.

LONDON:

Printed for J. ALMON, oppofite Burlington-Houfe in Piccadilly.

MDCCLXIX.

[Price One Shilling.]

ADVERTISEMENT.

MINUTES of the following Speech having been taken at the time it was made, and some copies having been handed about, one of them fell into the possession of the publisher; but before he would offer it to the public, he submitted it to the perusal of some Gentlemen, who had heard the Speech delivered, and whose accurate and retentive memories have supplied every defect in the minutes. He can therefore now venture to vouch for its authenticity; and assures the public, it is really and literally what the title imports it to be, The Speech of a right honourable Gentleman, upon the motion for expelling Mr. Wilkes *the first time* from his seat in the present parliament for the county of Middlesex. Though at the same time he is bound in justice to inform them, that it is published without the approbation, consent, or knowledge, of the Right Honourable Gentleman who made it.

To prevent the reader from confounding the subsequent proceedings against Mr. Wilkes with that which gave occasion to this Speech, the fatal consequences of which are therein so clearly predicted, it may be proper to remark, that Mr. Wilkes was first elected for the county of Middlesex, on the 28th day of March, 1768; that he was expelled on the 3d of February, 1769, the day on which this Speech was delivered; that he was rechosen for Middlesex the 16th day of the same month; that his election was declared void, and himself declared incapable of being elected into the present parliament, on the 17th day of the same month; that he was again elected on the 16th day of March, when no other candidate appeared, except Mr. Dingly, who had not one vote; that his election was again declared void on the 17th day of the same month; that on the 13th day of April he was returned by the sheriffs, as having 1143 votes, and Col. Luttrell only 296. That on the 15th day of the same month, the House of Commons voted, " That Mr. Luttrell *ought* to have been returned;" and that Gentleman took his seat accordingly. That a Petition from several freeholders of the county of Middlesex having been presented against Mr. Luttrell on the 29th day of April, the House of Commons voted, on the 8th of May, " That Henry Lawes Luttrell, Esq; " is duly elected a Knight of the Shire, to serve in this " present Parliament, for the County of Middlesex."

S P E E C H,

ON THE

MOTION for Expelling Mr. WILKES,

Friday, February 3, 1769.

Motion made by Lord Barrington, *and seconded by Mr.* Rigby.

THAT John Wilkes, Esq; a member of this House, who hath at the Bar of this House confessed himself to be the Author and Publisher of what this House has resolved to be an insolent, scandalous, and seditious Libel, and who has been convicted in the Court of King's Bench, of having Printed and Published a Seditious Libel, and three obscene and impious Libels, and by the judgment of the said Court has been sentenced to undergo twenty-two Months Imprisonment, and is now in Execution under the said Judgment, be expelled this House.

Mr. Speaker,

I have endeavoured to form my judgment with regard to this Question, which was not unexpected, upon the fullest and most impartial consideration; and having done so, I do not think myself obliged to make the least apology to any individual, or body

B   of

of men whatsoever, for the opinion which I shall deliver upon this subject.

I should indeed have wished that I could with propriety have declined delivering my sentiments concerning it, because I am thoroughly sensible that whatever my opinion shall be, it will be liable to great misconstructions and misrepresentations, both within these walls and without doors. If I give my vote for the motion as it was made to you, it will be said, that I do it from a cruel unrelenting disposition, to gratify a private and personal resentment for the abuse Mr. Wilkes has so liberally thrown upon me, and for that purpose under the mask of zeal for the cause of God and of the King, to persevere in loading an unhappy man, who, it has been frequently said in this House, has been already too severely oppressed by my means, or at least with my concurrence; or it would perhaps be attributed, especially after the temperate conduct which I have endeavoured to hold during this session, to an abject flattery to power, with the mean paltry view of obtaining court favour. On the other hand, if I give my vote against the expulsion of Mr. Wilkes, I shall be charged with levity and inconsistency, with changing my opinions as it may best suit my situation either in or out of office, with adopting new principles from new habitudes and connections, and with a factious design of courting popularity, and distressing all

legal

legal government, by fupporting and pro-
tecting a man, whofe behaviour I had fo repeatedly and fo heavily cenfured. If I know
my own failings, revenge and cruelty are
among the vices to which I am leaft incli-
ned; and if I may truft to the reproaches
thrown out againft me by my enemies, I
have been often accufed of obftinacy and
inflexibility of temper, but feldom or never
I think with being too much difpofed to al-
ter my opinions according to the will of
others, or to fail along the tide of popular
prejudice. I fhould flatter myfelf therefore,
that the charge of facrificing principles to
court favour or popular applaufe, could not
with juftice be applied to me, notwithftanding which I will again freely own, that I
fhould have wifhed for many reafons not to
have been under the neceffity of deciding
upon this Queftion, either one way or the
other. But as it has been propofed to you,
I think it would be a bafe and unworthy
conduct meanly to hide my head or to run
away from the difficulty. On the contrary,
it is the duty of every honeft man, if he is
convinced that the judgment which he has
formed is a right one, to declare it publicly
in his place, to abide by it, and boldly to
face any difficulties which may encounter it.
I am under no reftraint either from this or
that fide of the Houfe, I know and feel my
own independence on both, and while I continue here, I will exert it, and upon this

occafion

occafion execute an office greater than any
which the wildeft applaufe of the multitude
can give, or than the King himfelf can be-
ftow, greater than the office of First Com-
miffioner of the Treafury, or either of the
Secretaries of State: the honourable and
noble office of fpeaking the truth, and of doing impartial juftice. I will not palliate
this man's offences, or try to move your
compaffion: for that would be to appeal to
your weaknefs againft your judgment, much
lefs will I inveigh againft him in bitter terms,
and ftrive to excite your indignation: for
inftead of your weaknefs I fhould then apply
to your wicked paffions. With thefe fentiments I fhall proceed to the immediate
examination of the Queftion before you.
And in the firft place, I cannot agree with
thofe who have urged in behalf of Mr.
Wilkes, that this motion ought not to be
complied with, becaufe he is already the
moft unhappy, as well as the moft oppreffed
and injured man that this age has feen: he
is indeed unhappy, becaufe he is guilty, and
guilt muft ever produce unhappinefs; but
in other refpects, confidering his repeated
offences, he has certainly been more fortu-
nate, than his moft fanguine wifhes could
have expected. I mean not to enter into
the detail of all that has happened to him,
it would carry me too far, but to juftify
what I have faid, let me afk a few queftions.
When he wrote that feditious libel againft
the

the King and both Houfes of Parliament,
could he forefee that he fhould be taken up
by a General Warrant, againft the declared
opinion and defire of the two Secretaries of
State, who repeatedly propofed to have his
name inferted in the warrant of apprehenfion, but were overuled by the lawyers and
clerks of the office, who infifted they could
not depart from the long eftablifhed precedents and courfe of proceedings. Could
Mr. Wilkes forefee, that after an hundred
years practice, under the eye of the greateft
lawyers, before the fupreme courts of juftice, without being ever queftioned in one
fingle inftance, that this irregularity and il-
legality would be firft found out in his cafe,
and afterwards adopted by the voice and
clamour of the people upon the occafion of
his apprehenfion ? Had he been tried and
convicted without this irregularity, what
wou'd have been his fituation, and where
his popularity and the liberal fupport which
he has met with ? What would have become of the large damages which he has already obtained by this means, or the im-
menfe fums which he now fues for, and on
which he places his laft dependance ? Are
thefe the proofs that he has been the moft
unfortunate, or is it more true that he has
been the moft oppreffed and injured man
this age has feen. Dr. Shebbeare was taken up by a General Warrant from the Se-
cretary of State, dated 12 January, 1758,

conceived

conceived word for word in the fame terms, for writing the fixth letter to the people of England on the progrefs of national ruin, in which is fhewn, that the prefent grandeur of France and calamities of this nation are owing to the influence of Hanover on the councils of England. Under this General Warrant all his papers were feized as in the cafe of Mr. Wilkes, and he was profecuted for this offence by Mr. Pratt, then Attorney General, now Lord Chancellor of Great Britain. He was tried and convicted of it on the 17th of May, and on the 28th of November following he was fentenced to be fined, to ftand in the pillory, to be imprifoned for three years, and then to give fecurity for his good behaviour for feven years. The profecution againft Mr. Wilkes was directed by the unanimous addrefs of both Houfes of Parliament. He was tried and convicted by a favourable jury, for a libel certainly not lefs feditious or criminal than Dr. Shebbeare's. He was fentenced to be fined five hundred pounds, and to be imprifoned for one year inftead of three years, to give fecurity for his good behaviour for feven years, and the ignominious part of the punifhment was wholly remitted. He was tried and convicted likewife for being the author and publifher of the three obfcene and impious libels, upon a profecution directed in confequence of an addrefs from the Houfe of Lords, for which he

received

received exactly the fame fentence as for the former offence, including the two months imprifonment, which he had fuffered before judgment was given. Was he for either of thefe offences, or indeed for all of them taken together, fo feverely dealt with as Dr. Shebbeare for one alone. I do not go any further back, tho' a multitude of fimilar inftances, and fome more fevere even than that of Dr. Shebbeare might be produced within thefe laft forty or fifty years. What I have already mentioned feems to me fully fufficient to fhew, that Mr. Wilkes is not entitled to any extraordinary favour on the prefent occafion, from the plea of his having been the object of extraordinary feverity during the courfe of the former proceedings. But, though not to favour, yet he is moft certainly entitled to that juftice which is due to every man, and which we ought to be more particularly careful to preferve, in an inftance where paffion and prejudice may both concur in the violation of it. Thefe are principles which no one will difpute with me, and in confequence of them, after having thoroughly confidered the charge contained in your Queftion, and the arguments urged in fupport of it, I am clearly of opinion, that I ought not to give my affent to the propofition which has been made to you; becaufe if I did, I fhould thereby commit a capital injuftice. I am fenfible that the expreffion is a ftrong one, and that it is incumbent upon me to

fhew

shew my reasons for applying it to the motion now under your consideration, which I shall endeavour to do as fully and as satisfactorily as I am able.

I perfectly agree with the gentleman * who has told you, that this House has a right to enquire into the conduct of its members, and that they have exercised that right in a great variety of instances, in which they have tried, censured and expelled them according to the established course of our proceedings, and the law of Parliament, which is part of the law of the Kingdom. Let us examine the proposition now before you by this rule, and we shall then be able to judge, whether it is conformable to the usage and law of parliament, to the practice of any other court of justice in the kingdom, or to the unalterable principles of natural equity, or whether it is a new and dangerous mode of proceeding, unsupported by any precedent or example in the Journals of parliament, or the records of any other court, calculated merely to serve a present purpose, and as such, well deserving the term which I gave to it of a capital injustice. The charge contained in this motion consists of four articles, each of which it has been contended is sufficient singly to justify the conclusion drawn from them all put together, that Mr. Wilkes ought to be expelled. Upon this complicated charge, the House is now called upon to give a judgment for or against the question.

It

It is a well known and undeniable rule in this House, founded in common sense, that, whenever a question, even of the most trivial nature, is complicated, and contains different branches, every individual Member, has an indubitable right to have the question separated, that he may not be obliged to approve or disapprove in the lump, but that every part of the proposition should stand or fall abstractedly upon its own merits. I need not shew the propriety and the absolute necessity for this; it is so self evident, that every argument I could urge in support of it would only weaken it. And surely if it holds good in all cases where we act only in a deliberative capacity, it will not be contended, that it is less true, or less necessary, when we are to exercise our judicial powers, when we are to censure and to punish, and to affect not only the rights of our own member, but the franchises of those who sent him hither as their representative. I may safely challenge the gentlemen, the most knowing in the Journals of this House, to produce a single precedent of a similar nature. And if none shall be produced, as I am convinced there cannot, am I not founded in saying, that this is a new attempt, unsupported by law and usage of parliament.

But this mode of proceeding is not only new and unprecedented, it is likewise dangerous and unjust. For the proof of it, let me recall to your minds what has passed in

C   the

the courſe of this debate ; one very learned
kſtone and worthy gentleman *, who ſpoke early,
declared, that he gave his conſent to this
motion for expulſion, upon that article of
the charge alone, which relates to the three
obſcene and impious libels, diſavowing, in
the moſt direct terms, all the other articles,
becauſe he thought, that the libel relative
to Lord Weymouth's letter was not properly and regularly brought before us, and that
Mr. Wilkes, having been already expelled
by a former parliament, for the ſeditious libel of the North Briton, ought not to be
puniſhed and expelled a ſecond time by a
ſubſequent parliament for the ſame offence.
His argument was, that the former Houſe of
Commons, having vindicated the honour of
the King and of Parliament, he hoped this
Houſe would not ſhew leſs zeal to vindicate
the cauſe of God and of Religion. He ſpoke
with a becoming zeal and indignation, rai-
ſed, as he told us, by having read ſome of
the wicked and impious expreſſions contained in the Record now upon your table. His
opinions (which were ſoon after followed
by another learned gentleman †, who adopted the ſame train of reaſoning) joined to
the ſerious manner in which he delivered
them, ſeemed to make great impreſſion upon the Houſe, and tho' I differ with him in
his concluſion, yet I agree with him in his
principles, and was glad to ſee this offence
treated as it ought to be. For, if we treat

it

it with mirth and levity, we in some measure
justify the libel itself by our conduct, and
share the guilt of the author. On the other
hand, what were the arguments of the two
noble lords*, who spoke lately for the expulsion? They agreed indeed with the learned gentlemen in the conclusion, but differ-
ed widely in the premises with regard to
the articles of the charge on which they
founded their judgment. They both dif-
claimed the article of the three obscene and
impious libels as any ground for this proceeding. They expressed their disapproba-
tion of the manner in which the copy of
them was obtained from Mr. Wilkes's ser-
vant, and their doubts with regard to his
intention to publish them. One of them
therefore desired to draw a veil over that part
of the charge, that it might no more be
mentioned, and the other wished to bury the
whole of that transaction in oblivion. The
first, waving the rest of the charge, grounded
his assent to the motion upon the seditious
libel of the North Briton; the latter, if I
mistake not, upon the libel against lord
Weymouth. These sentiments likewise
seemed to meet with great approbation from
many of your members. Another gentleman †, who is very conversant in the Journals of the House, and could not therefore
but be sensible both of the novelty and
danger of this proceeding upon such an accumulated and complicated charge, thought

* Lord Frederick Campbell, Lord Palmerston.

† Mr. Dylon.

it

it neceſſary to take a different ground. He
ſeemed to wave the criminal parts of the
charge, but inſiſted ſtrongly upon Mr.
Wilkes's incapacity of continuing a member
of Parliament, ariſing from his impriſon-
ment, which the Houſe had declared to be
no caſe of privilege, and from which they
could not therefore diſcharge him.

I have ſtated theſe arguments, and I appeal to the Houſe, whether I have miſre-
preſented them. I might in the ſame manner go thro' the reſt of this debate; I think
not above two gentlemen, who have ſpoken
together, have agreed in aſſigning the ſame
offence as the proper ground for this expulſion. It is impoſſible to form any judgment
concerning the ſentiments of thoſe who
have not ſpoken, except from thoſe who
have, and from the approbation which has
been given to what they declared. If I am
to judge from thence, I ſhould imagine, that
the opinions of thoſe who concur in this
queſtion of expulſion, are almoſt equally di-
vided among the ſeveral branches of the
charge contained in it; but however that
may be, it is undeniably true, that great
numbers of gentlemen approve of ſome
parts of the charge, and diſapprove of others,
and ſo, *vice verſâ*. What then may be the
conſequence of blending the whole of this
matter together? Is it not evident, that by
this unworthy artifice, Mr. Wilkes may be
expelled, although three parts in four of
those

thofe who expell him fhould have declared
againſt his expulfion upon every one of the
articles contained in this charge. Would
not this fevere punifhment be inflicted upon
him, in that cafe, by a minority, againſt the
fenfe and judgment of a great majority of
this Houfe? To explain this in a manner
obvious to the apprehenfion of every gentleman who hears me, let me fuppofe, that an
indictment were framed, confifting of four
diftinct offences, each inferring the penalty of
death; charging for example that the prifoner on the firſt of May had committed trea-
fon, on the firſt of June murther, on the
firſt of July robbery, and on the firſt of
Auguft forgery. Let me fuppofe any court
of judicature in the kingdom ignorant and
wicked enough to admit of, and to try the
prifoner upon fuch a complicated indictment, notwithftanding any objection he
could make to it. Might he not be found
guilty of each of thefe offences by three different jurymen, and declared innocent by
nine, and would he not in fact by this contri-
vance be condemned to death by three, although acquitted by nine? What would
mankind, what would you yourfelves fay of
fuch a fentence fo obtained? Would you
not think the term of capital injuftice too
foft an expreffion? Would you not call it
the worft of murthers, a murther under the
colour of law and juftice? The punifhment
would indeed be different, becaufe the offences

fences are fo, but the mode of proceeding on the prefent occafion is exactly the fame, and equally inconfiftent with the law and ufage of parliament, with the practice of every court of judicature in any civilized country, and with the unalterable principles of natural equity. But I will reftrain my expreffions, and leave this part of the Quef-tion to your own feelings, which I am per-fuaded will enforce it more ftrongly than any arguments of mine.

I have hitherto taken the whole of this complicated charge together, and have fhown the dangerous confequences refulting from it; I will now unravel the web, and con-fider the different parts of it feparately and diftinctly. The firft which prefents itfelf is the libel relative to Lord Weymouth's letter, which has been new chriftened for this fpe-cial purpofe. It was complained of in the other Houfe as a breach of privilege, and as a grofs and impudent libel, which it certain-ly is, againft a peer of the realm, and one of his Majefty's principal fecretaries of ftate. But when it appeared to be written by Mr. Wilkes, it was to change its name and its nature. The particular complaint and all mention of the noble Lord concerned in it was to be dropped, and it became at once a matter of fedition againft the ftate. With what view was this alteration made? Why did not the Houfe of Lords addrefs the King, to have it profecuted by the Attorney Ge-neral,

neral, in the fame manner as was done with regard to the three obfcene and impious libels which were written by the fame perfon then a member of this Houfe, and were likewife complained of as a breach of privilege againft a peer of parliament? What was the motive for this difference of proceeding in the other Houfe, on two offences of the fame nature againft the fame perfon? It was not out of regard to us and to our privileges, for they well knew, that we had joined with them in a folemn declaration, that in this cafe there was no privilege, and they themfelves had proceeded in confequence of it againft this very man then a member of Parliament, for a fimilar offence, without communicating it to the Houfe of Commons. Can any reafon be affigned for this, except a defire in their Lordfhips to fhift the jurifdiction, and inftead of fending it to the courts of law, where libels againft minifters have hitherto always been tried, to tranfmit it to us to be punifhed, contrary to all precedent and example, by an extraordinary extenfion of our judicature? And will this Houfe, whofe peculiar duty it is to watch over and to guard the laws of the land from all encroachments, and who have looked with the moft jealous eye upon every act which has the leaft tendency to exempt the peers of the realm, and their caufes from that jurifdiction which is common to all, will this

this Houfe, I fay, lend its name to fuch an evafion, and extend its judicature for fuch a purpofe? fhall we take upon ourfelves fo odious an office, and anfwer fuch a demand at fight, with no other view, than to fave their Lordfhips the difficulty and obloquy, which is the ufual confequence of thefe profecutions? If this attempt fhould fucceed, and fo eafy and fummary a method fhould be marked out for the punifhment of thofe who fhall libel minifters of ftate, this probably will not be the laft application which we fhall receive of this nature. We have enough to do, too much I fear, to maintain our own authority and dignity unimpeached, and furely the other Houfe has fufficient power in themfelves, with the affiftance of the courts of law, to vindicate their members from every infult.

The next article is that of the feditious libel the North Briton, for which, the author and publifher was defervedly profecuted, tried and convicted five years ago, in confequence of the unanimous addrefs of both Houfes of Parliament. He was likewife expelled by the laft Houfe of Commons for the indignity offered to *them* by one of their own members, of which *they* were the only judges, and which they alone could punifh; a cafe fo widely different from that of a libel on any particular perfon or minifter of ftate, that it is quite unneceffary to do more than to mark it out to your obfervation.

For

For this libel of the North Briton Mr.
Wilkes has been fentenced, and is now un-
dergoing the punifhment inflicted on him
by Law. He has likewife been punifhed
by expulfion from the former Houfe of Commons for the particular offence committed
againft them. There is not a rule more
facred in the jurifprudence of this country,
than that a man once acquitted or condemned,
fhall not be tried or punifhed again *by the
fame judicature* for the fame offence. How
many notorious criminals daily efcape by the
ftrict obfervance of this rule, and yet the
principle of it is fo falutary, and fo deeply
rooted in the minds of men, that no one
dares to fet his face againft it, and to avow
an intention to break through it. It was
but a few days ago that I fpoke and voted
to reftrain Mr. Wilkes from entering into the
greater part of his petition, becaufe the
fubject matter of his complaint had been
fully heard, and the parties to it duly acquitted by the laft Houfe of Commons.
The Houfe, after long debate, adopted the
reafoning, and Mr. Wilkes was reftrained
accordingly.

And fhall I, within the little fpace of a
few days, forget every argument which I
then ufed againft him, and declare without
fhame that the fame rule of law, which was
conclufive when urged in behalf of his ad-
verfaries, fhould in the fame caufe be of no
avail when pleaded in his favour. Is this

D   that

that confiftency upon which I, and thofe who hear me, are to value ourfelves? I have not taken up that facred principle fo lightly, nor will I fo wantonly depart from it. Permit me to give you an inftance of it. Many years ago, a propofition was made to allow of a revifion of the fentence of a court martial. The Queftion was folemnly argued. I then fat at the treafury board with a minifter* for whom I had the higheft perfonal regard and refpect; and yet in oppofition to him, and to the fentiments of thofe †, with whom I was connected by the neareft ties both of blood and friendfhip, I repeatedly voted and fpoke againft that revifion, in conjunction with a noble perfon ‡, who then fat at the fame board with me, and an honourable gentleman ‖, an officer of the army, who afterwards held the office of one of his Majefty's Principal Secretaries of State, who now hears me, and to whom I appeal for the truth of what I have faid upon this fubject. Is not this the revifion of a fentence given in a former parliament in order to encreafe it? And if this motion for the expulfion of Mr. Wilkes, as grounded upon that offence, fhall prevail, will he not be twice expelled and twice punifhed for one crime by the fame judicature, in direct violation of that falutary principle, to the truth of which we ourfelves have fo lately affented.

The

* Mr. Pelham.

† Lord Temple and Lord Chatham.

‡ Lord Lyttelton.

‖ General Conway.

The third article contained in the charge is for Printing and Publiſhing three impious and obſcene Libels, under the title of the Eſſay upon Woman; I truſt that none who hear me, I am ſure that no one who knows me will believe, that I mean to palliate that crime, or the ſeditious and dangerous Libel which I have juſt now mentioned. I will go further, I cannot agree with thoſe who think, that the papers relative to it were obtain'd by thoſe who proſecuted him in any undue or improper manner. The contrary has appeared by Mr. Wilkes's own evidence a few days ago. That Proſecution was begun in another place, and I had nothing to do with it; but in juſtice to thoſe who were concerned, I muſt ſay, that there was not the leaſt foundation for all that calumny that has been propagated with regard to the manner of obtaining them, for the truth of which I appeal to the examination which the Houſe has ſo lately made on Mr. Wilkes's petition upon that ſubject. I muſt therefore freely declare, that this obſervation has no weight with me. The other part of the objection is founded upon the evidence given at your Bar, that Mr. Wilkes had directed only 12 copies of them to be printed, and had ſtrictly ordered, that they ſhould all be delivered into his own hands, from whence it is urged, that he had no intention to publiſh them at large. This may be indeed a circumſtance of alleviation,

which

which I am the more authorifed to fay, as I am informed it was mentioned by the *learned judge* *, in mitigation of the fentence given againft him in the court of King's Bench. But the ftrongeft plea in his defence upon this head is, that the crime was committed five years ago, that the law has already punifhed it, that the laft Houfe of Commons, though they were not ignorant of it when they proceeded againft him, and certainly were not partial to him, yet, as they were not particularly concerned in it, did not think it right for them to interfere in it. It might therefore be thought a hardfhip to him to let it pafs unnoticed by them, and many years after to transfer it to another parliament, and to referve it in fo unufual a manner for a frefh cenfure.

The laft article of this complicated charge is, that Mr. Wilkes has been fentenced by the judgment of the court of King's Bench to undergo twenty-two months imprifonment, and that he is now in execution under that judgment. This circumftance has been principally relied upon and enforced by a gentleman †, who has labour'd very ftrongly to prove that, as Mr. Wilkes is thereby difabled from taking his feat, and doing his duty for fixteen months to come, this difability alone is a proper and fufficient ground to juftify the propofition which has been made to you for expelling him. You have been told very truly, that his conftituents

have

* Mr. Juftice Yates.

† Mr. Dyfon.

have the cleareft and moft undeniable right
to the attendance of their reprefentatives in
parliament, that there is no privilege which
we are or ought to be fo tender of as to free
our members from the leaft reftraint, which
may prevent or even interrupt them in the
exercife of this duty, that this confideration is
of fuch infinite moment, that the ufual courfe
of juftice in all civil cafes is to give way to
it and be fufpended, in order to preferve the
right of our conftituents from being violated
in the fmalleft degree : that we have already
declared, that Mr. Wilkes is not entitled by
privilege of parliament to be difcharged from
his imprifonment, and that we have no other
method to enforce the attendance of our
member : that under thefe circumftances he
would for a long time to come be utterly difabled from performing that duty which he
owes to his conftituents, unlefs the king
fhould be pleafed to pardon him, which
would in effect be leaving to the option of
the crown to determine, whether one of our
members fhould or fhould not take his feat
in this Houfe. I entirely concur with the
general pofitions which have been laid down
as the foundation of this argument, but I
differ extremely in the confequences which
have been drawn from it, and think that I
can fhew to a demonftration, that by the
law and conftant ufage of parliament, the
inability of attending his duty for the fpace
of a year or two has never been deemed a
fufficient

sufficient reason for the expulsion of a member. I say his inability, for his imprisonment has justly been stated, not as a fresh crime, but as an inability in him to attend, and in the House to reclaim him. The proposition therefore is, that whenever a member is restrained from doing his duty here, and that the House cannot compel his attendance without the immediate interposition and consent of the Crown, in all such cases the House is bound by the law and practice of parliament to proceed to an expulsion of the member so disabled.

Let us see how far this doctrine is warranted by former precedents. Not one has been produced in support of it. On the contrary, need I put that gentleman in mind of a multitude of examples, many of which have happened in our own time, which prove the very reverse of it. Does he not remember the case of lord Barrymore and Sir John Douglas, both of them members of this House, who were imprisoned upon the suspension of the Habeas Corpus Act for a longer period of time than Mr. Wilkes, and who could not be deliver'd from that imprisonment without the interposition and consent of the Crown? many cases of a similar nature must be fresh in the memory of us all, but there is one which I cannot mention without a particular respect and reverence to the person concerned in it. I mean the case of Sir William Wyndham.

He

He was imprifoned in the Tower for upwards of two years, during which time the
county which he reprefented, and the public in general, were deprived of thofe fervices for which he was fo eminently qualified, and which he performed with fo much
honour to himfelf and advantage to them.
But though the times were warm and vio-
lent, and many wifhed to get rid of thofe
abilities which they were well acquainted
with, yet no man ventured in that or any
of the other inftances to maintain the doctrine now laid down, that becaufe the parties were reftrained from their attendance
here by a legal imprifonment, from which
this Houfe could not deliver them without
the interpofition and confent of the Crown,
they therefore ought by the law and conftitution of Parliament to be expelled. I am
well aware that in thefe cafes it may be faid,
the parties had not been convicted, that
there is therefore a great difference as to the
certainty of the crime imputed to them. It
is true, and God forbid that I fhould draw
any parallel of that kind, but with regard
to the reftraint abftracted from the crime,
which is made the only foundation of this
part of the argument, it is exactly the fame
as in the prefent inftance. Nor will the confequences ftop here, if it fhould be admitted that this argument is well founded; I
am convinced the gentleman who urged it
was not aware of them. Would he wifh
that

that all thofe whom the king can by law
reftrain from their attendance in this Houfe
for the fpace of 15 or 16 months, and who
are thereby unable to difcharge the duty
which they owe to their conftituents.
Would he wifh, I fay, that they fhould be
all declared, ipfo facto, incapable of fitting
in parliament after that reftraint fhall be
ended; has he forgotten how many officers,
both in the land and fea fervice, whilft they
were members of this Houfe, were abfent
for many years together, during the late
war? Are there not many in the fame
fituation, who are at this very time actually
employed upon military fervices in our gar-
rifons abroad? Can they leave that duty
without the interpofition and confent of the
Crown; or, if they cannot, will it be contended, that they are difabled from ever re-
turning amongft us, and that their feats
are thereby vacated. This doctrine, if true,
would prove, that the gentlemen of the Army and of the Navy, who from the nature
and condition of the refpective fervices, are
at all times liable to this objection, are for
that reafon not eligible into this Houfe, and
would be the ftrongeft argument for an act
of parliament declaring their incapacity.
Many other cafes might be put of tempora-
ry difabilities, even for a longer fpace of
time, which have never been, and I believe
never will be deemed proper grounds for an
expulfion. I fhall not however ftate them

parti-

particularly, becaufe thofe which I have already ftated will furely be fufficient to con- vince the Houfe, that this propofition is di- rectly contrary to the practice, and that it has never been warranted in any one inftance by the law and ufage of parliament.

But it has been urged, whatever may be the cafe in point of form, with regard to the feveral articles contained in this queftion, whether taken together as an accumulated and complicated charge, or confidered fepa- rately and diftinctly, yet this Houfe muft neceffarily be the judges, whether any mem- ber of their own is or is not a fit perfon to fit amongft them, and it has been argued, that if the laft parliament thought him un- fit, the prefent has certainly an equal right to adjudge that he is fo. It has been afked, what merit has he had fince that time to recommend him, and to induce the prefent parliament to think him a properer man to fit amongft them, than he was to fit among their predeceffors. This would indeed be a conclufive argument, if we really had that difcretionary power of excluding all thofe whom we think improper upon which it is founded. But we have no fuch general au- thority vefted in us, nor is there a fingle precedent where we have pretended to exer- cife it. Whenever this Houfe has expelled any member, it has invariably affign'd fome particular offence as the reafon for fuch ex- pulfion. By the fundamental principles of

E   this

this conftitution, the right of judging upon
the general propriety or unfitnefs of their
reprefentatives is entrufted with the electors, and when chofen, this Houfe can
only exclude or expell them for fome difability eftablifhed by the law of the land,
or for fome fpecific offence alledged and
proved. If it were otherwife, we fhould in
fact elect ourfelves, inftead of being chofen
by our refpective conftituents. If I had
been one of the electors for the county of
Middlefex, I fhould have fhown by my
vote the opinion which I entertained with
regard to the conduct and character of Mr.
Wilkes, and to the propriety of choofing
him a knight of the fhire for that county.
I had not only a right, but it would have
been my duty to have manifefted that opinion. But when he is chofen and returned
hither; my duty is widely different. We
are now acting in our judicial capacity, and
are therefore to found the judgment which
we are to give, not upon our wifhes and in-
clinations, not upon our private belief or
arbitrary opinions, but upon fpecific facts
alledged and proved according to the eftablifhed rules and courfe of our proceedings.
When we are to act as judges, we are not
to affume the characters of legiflators, any
more than the Court of King's Bench, who
were bound to reverfe Mr. Wilkes's outlawry if they found any irregularity in it, tho'
poffibly they were convinced in their
private

private opinions, that it would have been more beneficial to the state to have confirmed it. If we depart from this principle, and allow to ourselves a latitude of judging in questions of this nature, if we are to admit those whom we think most proper, and to expell those whom we think most improper, to what lengths will not this doctrine carry us? There never was a parliament chosen, into which there were not some persons elected whom the greater part of the House thought unworthy of that honour. I speak of former parliaments, and it becomes us to be careful that posterity should not speak still worse of us. Let me suppose for a moment, that this were true, to a certain degree even in the present parliament, and that it were carried still farther from party prejudice, or from motives less defensible. This would indeed be the sure means of purging the House effectually from all ill humours within these walls, and of dispersing them at the same time through every corner of the kingdom. But if this summary mode of reasoning was really meant to be adopted, there was certainly no occasion for our sitting four or five days and nights together, to decide a question, which might as well have been determined in so many minutes. I cannot therefore bring myself to think, that any gentleman will avow the proposition to this extent. But perhaps some may wish to shelter themselves

E 2   under

under the other part of the argument, and
may contend, that a Man who has been expelled by a former House of Commons cannot, at least in the judgment of those who
concurred in that sentence, be deemed a
proper person to sit in the present parliament, unless he has some pardon to plead,
or some merit to cancel his former offences.
They will find upon examination that this
doctrine is almost as untenable as the other.
Votes of censure, and even commitments by
either House of Parliament acting in that
capacity only, determine, as it is well known,
with the session.   There are indeed some instances, where in matters of contempt and
refusal to submit to the orders of the House,
the proceeding has been taken up again in
a following session.   But to transfer an expulsion from one parliament to another,
and by this means to establish a perpetual
incapacity in the party so expelled, which
must be the consequence of it, as this objection will hold equally strong in any future parliament as in the present.   This I
say, would be contrary to all precedent and
example, and inconsistent with the spirit of
the constitution.   I could cite many precedents to prove the first part of my assertion, but
one alone will be sufficient for my purpose,
because that is so signal, and so memorable
in all its circumstances, as to render any
confirmation or inforcement of it quite unne-
cessary.   In quoting this precedent I beg
leave

leave to fay, that I do not intend to throw
any imputation on any perfon whatfoever.
I neither mean to acquit or to condemn thofe
who were parties to it, but merely to ftate
the fact as it appears from your journals,
and then to fubmit the refult of it to the
judgment of thofe who hear me. The cafe
I allude to was that of Mr. Walpole, who
was afterwards firft minifter to king George
the Firft and king George the Second for
the term of twenty years and upwards. On
the 17th of January 17$\frac{11}{12}$ he was voted
by the Houfe of Commons guilty of a high
breach of truft and notorious corruption, in
receiving the fum of 500 guineas, and taking
a note for 500 pounds more on account of
two contracts made by him when fecretary
at war, purfuant to a power granted by the
lord treafurer, and for this offence he was
committed prifoner to the Tower and expelled the Houfe. He was immediately re-
elected, but declared incapable of being
chofen during that parliament. However,
on the diffolution of it a year and a half afterwards, he was again chofen into the new
parliament, was admitted to take his feat
without the leaft queftion or objection on
account of his former expulfion, and continued a Member of the Houfe of Commons in every fubfequent parliament till the
year 1742, when he was created earl of Or-
ford. It cannot be denied that the offence
was in its nature infamous, and fuch a one

as

as rendered the person guilty of it unfit to
be trusted with the power to give, or to
manage the public money. The same
party that expelled him, whose enmity was
aggravated by his great talents and knowledge of business, continued equally ad-
verse to him, and equally prevalent in the
new parliament; but however desirous they
were to get rid of him, and however vio-
lent upon many other occasions, yet in the
very zenith of their power, they did not
dare to set up this pretence, or to urge the
expulsion of a former parliament, although
not two years before, as a sufficient ground
for re-expelling or declaring him incapable
of sitting in a new parliament. If this
could have been attempted, every circumstance concurred to make them wish it. The
crime itself was breach of trust, and notorious corruption in a public officer relative
to public money, an offence in the eye of
parliament certainly not less infamous or
less criminal than writing and publishing
a seditious libel. Few if any were more
obnoxious, or more formidable to them
than the gentleman who had been the object of their justice or resentment. The
heat of party rage had been pleaded
in excuse, if not in justification of many
extravagancies on both sides, but they
thought this measure beyond the mark of a
common violence, and therefore dared not
to attempt it. I have said before, that it
was

was not my intention to approve or to blame
the cenfure then paffed upon that extraordinary man. It was the fubject of great
difcuffion and altercation at the time. I do
not wifh to revive paft heats. The prefent
are more than fufficient, and all wife and
good men fhould endeavour by juftice and
moderation to allay them. Let us therefore
take it either way. Let us fuppofe, that he
was guilty or innocent of the charge to the
utmoft extent, and then let us confider how
the cafe will apply to that part of the
queftion which is now before us. The
crime, as it related to a fraud concerning
the public revenue, was certainly under the
immediate cognizance of this Houfe, and
was perhaps punifhable in no other manner.
They punifhed it as feverely as they could,
both by imprifonment and expulfion; the
former of which ended in a few months, and
the confequences of the latter in a year and
an half. If he was guilty of a high breach
of truft and notorious corruption, he was
certainly very unfit to be invefted with the
moft facred truft in the kingdom, that of a
member of the legiflature. Had the Queftion been afked upon that occafion likewife,
what merit he had after his firft expulfion to
recommend him to the fubfequent parliament? The anfwer muft have been, that he
had perfifted in juftifying what he had
done, that he had appealed not only to his
electors, but to the world at large in more
than

than one printed pamphlet, accufing the
Houfe of Commons which had condemned
him, of violence and injuftice. With all
thefe aggravations, and with every other in-
ducement, what could have protected him,
what could have prevented his re-expulfion,
but the notoriety and the certainty that fuch a
meafure was not confiftent with the known law
and ufage of parliament, even when exerted
againft a guilty and obnoxious man? This is
the ftate of the argument upon that fuppofition; but if we take the other part of the
alternative, and fuppofe that he was innocent of the charge, the propofition would
be much ftronger; we muft then confider
him in the light of a man expelled by party
rage, or on worfe motives, not for his
crimes but for his merit, not that he was
unfit, but that he was too well qualified
for the truft repofed in him. What would
have been the confequence, if this doctrine
of transferring the difability incurred by a
former fentence to a fubfequent parliament
had been then eftablifhed? The public and
this Houfe would have been deprived for
ever of thofe fervices, which from his
knowledge and talents they had a right to
expect, and which they fo much relied upon, particularly in the important bufinefs
of the finances of this kingdom, and that
gentleman and his family would have been
precluded, irreparably precluded, by an unjuft judgment, from thofe great emoluments
and

and high honours which were conferred upon him by two fucceffive kings, as the re-
wards of his adminiftration. That lofs
however would have been the misfortune of
individuals, but a much heavier, a much
more extenfive misfortune would have be-
fallen the parliament and the conftitution,
if fo dangerous a precedent had taken place.
An eafy and effectual plan would have been
marked out to exclude from this Houfe for
ever, by an unjuft vote once paffed, any
member of it who fhould be obnoxious to
the rage of party, or to the wantonnefs of
power. Let not your prejudices, let not
your juft refentments againft the conduct
and character of the man, who is now the
object of our deliberation, prevail upon you
to ground any part of your proceedings upon fuch deftructive and fatal principles.
Confider that precedents of this nature are
generally begun in the firft inftance againft
the odious and the guilty, but when once
eftablifhed, are eafily applied to and made ufe
of againft the meritorious and the innocent:
that the moft eminent and beft deferving
members of the ftate, under the colour of
fuch an example, by one arbitrary and difcretionary vote of one Houfe of Parliament (the worft fpecies of Oftracifm) may
be excluded from the public councils, cut
off and profcribed from the rights of every
fubject of the realm, not for a term of
years alone, but for ever: that a claim of

F   this

this nature would be to assume to the majority of this House alone, the powers of the
whole legislature; for nothing short of their
united voice, declared by an act of parliament, has hitherto pretended to exercise
such a general discretion of punishing, contrary to the usual forms of law, and of en-
acting such a perpetual incapacity upon any
individual. There are indeed some instances
of the latter * kind in our statute books,
but even there they have been frequently
animadverted upon, and heavily censured
as acts of violence and injustice, and breaches
of the constitution. Let us remember the
well known observation of the learned and
sensible author of L'Esprit des Loix, who
states it as one of the excellencies of the
English constitution, of which he was a
professed admirer, " that the judicial pow-
" er is separated from the legislative;" and
tells us, " that there would be no liberty if
" they were blended together, that the
" power over the life and liberty of the
" citizens would then be arbitrary; for the
" judge would be the legislator." Shall we
then, who are the immediate delegated
guardians of that liberty and constitution,
shall we set the wicked example, and attempt to violate them to gratify our pas-
sions or our prejudices? And for whom
and upon what occasion? Not to preserve
the sacred person of sovereign from assassi-
nation, or his kingdoms from invasion or †
rebellion,

* Bills of Pains and Penalties.

† Fenwick and Atter-bury's Bills.

rebellion, not to defeat the arbitrary defigns of a defperate minifter or a defpotic court *, * Lord Strafford's Bill. but to inflict an additional punifhment upon a libeller, who appears by the queftion it-felf to have been convicted of the greater part of his offences by due courfe of law, and to be in actual imprifonment at this moment, under a legal fentence pronounced by the fupreme court of criminal juftice in confequence of that conviction. Can we fay, that there are not laws in being, to preferve the reverence due to the magiftrate, and to protect the dignity of the crown from fcandalous and feditious libels? Are they not fufficient, if temperately and firmly executed, to punifh and to deter the moft daring from the commiffion of thofe offences. If they are, for what purpofe is this application? If they are not, can the propofition now made to you be deemed the proper or the effectual method of enforcing them?

This brings me to the only part of the queftion which I have not yet touched upon; I mean the propriety and wifdom of this meafure; fuppofing even that it were clearly warranted by the law of the land, by the law and ufage of parliament, by the fpirit of our conftitution, and by the general principles of natural juftice: the contrary of which I think I have manifeftly fhown in every one of thofe particulars. What then are the motives of propriety and wif-

dom

dom by which we are called upon to come
into this extraordinary refolution ? I fhall
probably be told, that it is to check and to
reftrain the fpirit of faction and diforder, to
re-eftablifh the credit and authority of government, and to vindicate the honour of
this Houfe, by expreffing our abhorrence of
thefe offences.   No man has been more
defirous to attain thefe neceffary purpofes
than I have been, or will now fet his foot
farther for the accomplifhment of them by
all juft and legal means, in every inftance
confiftent with the public fafety.   I have
not changed my fentiments relative to Mr.
Wilkes, of whom I continue to think exactly in the fame manner as I have long
done ; but, whatever my fentiments are, it
cannot be denied, that he is now become
an object of popular favour.   Nor is that
popular favour confined to this capital, or
to its neighbourhood alone, but is extended
to the diftant parts of the kingdom.   The
temper of the people you have been truly
told, has on feveral occafions appeared to
be diforderly and licentious, fpurning at
the laws and at all lawful authority.   The
difficulties we have to ftruggle with, arifing
from the interior condition of this country,
from the difobedience of our colonies, and
from the ftate of our foreign affairs,   are
augmented to fuch a degree, as to form a
very dangerous crifis.   The refpect and reverence due to the parliament,   and the
confidence

confidence repofed in this Houfe, are vifibly diminifhed. Under thefe circumftances does it not behove us to be doubly cautious, not to exceed the ftricteft bounds of law and of the conftitution ? Is it not more advifeable, if the cafe can admit of a doubt, to conciliate the heated minds of men by temper and difcretion, than to inflame them by adding frefh fuel to difcontent ? Our fituation, I am fure, demands the firm fupport of an united people, and their affectionate reliance upon the wifdom of thofe who govern them. Till that can be reftored, at leaft in fome meafure, we may look around for order and for obedience in vain. If his Majefty's fervants can think that this proceeding is the likely means to reftore it, let them, for the fake of this Houfe, whofe exiftence depends upon the good opinion of our conftituents, as their happinefs does upon us; let them for their own fakes, confult that beft guide to all human wifdom, the experience of paft times; and where can they confult it more properly than in the hiftory of our own country. There they will find fome of the ableft minifters and the moft victorious general that any age could boaft of, difgraced and overturned in the midft of their fuccefs and triumph by a popular clamour of the danger of the church. The reverend incendiary Dr. Sacheverell, was unwifely profecuted by this Houfe. He became by that means the favourite and the

idol

idol of the people throughout England as much, nay more, than Mr. Wilkes is now. The Queen herself was ftopped and infulted in her chair during the trial, with God fave Dr. Sacheverell. I heartily wifh that no fimilar infult may have been offered to our prefent fovereign. The profecution went on and the ferment encreafed. The event verified a famous expreffion in thofe days, " that " the whigs had wifhed to roaft a parfon, and " that they had done it at fo fierce a fire, " that they had burnt themfelves," for the minifters were difmiffed, and the parliament diffolved. The reverend doctor, the mob idol, when he ceafed to be a martyr, foon funk into his original infignificancy, from which that martyrdom alone had raifed him. Mr. Wilkes, apprehenfive of the fame fate, and thoroughly fenfible, that the continuance . of his popularity will depend upon your conduct, ufes every means in his power to provoke you to fome inftance of unufual feverity. Suppofe that you could otherwife have doubted of it, yet his behaviour here at your bar, when called upon to juftify himfelf, is fully fufficient to prove the truth of what I have afferted. If he had intended to deprecate your refentment, and to ftop your proceedings againft him, he is not fo void of parts and underftanding, as to have told you in the words he ufed at the bar (when charged with writing the Libel againft lord Weymouth) " that he was only

forry

" forry he had not expreffed himfelf upon
" that fubject in ftronger terms, and that he
" certainly would do fo whenever a fimilar
" occafion fhould prefent itfelf ;" nor would
he have afked, " whether the precedents quo-
" ted by lord Mansfield were not all taken
" from the *Star Chamber*." If he had wifhed
to prevent his expulfion, he would have employed other methods to accomplifh his
purpofe ; but his object is not to retain his
feat in this Houfe, but to ftand forth to the
deluded people as the victim of your refentment, of your violence and injuftice.
This is the advantage which he manifeftly
feeks to derive from you, and will you be
weak enough to give it to him, and to fall
into fo obvious a fnare ? What benefit will
you gain, or what will he lofe, if this motion for his expulfion fhall take effect ?
Whatever talents he has to captivate or to
inflame the people without doors, he has
none to render him formidable within thefe
walls, or to combat the weighty and power-
ful arguments which minifters know how
to employ. He has holden forth high
founding and magnificent promifes of the
fignal fervices which he will perform to his
country in parliament, and there are many
who are ignorant and credulous enough to
believe them. Whenever he comes here,
I will venture to prophecy that they will be
grievoufly difappointed. That difappoint-
ment will be followed by difguft and anger,

at

at their having been fo grofsly deceived, and will probably turn the tide of popular pre-judice. But as foon as he fhall be excluded from this Houfe, they will give credit to him for more than he has even promifed. They will be perfuaded, that every real and ima-ginary grievance would have been redreffed by his patriotic care and influence. If in this fituation, any untoward accident, any diftrefs fhall befall us, the ferment will be encreafed by this circumftance, and the lan-guage of an uninformed and mifled people will be, " aye, if mafter Wilkes had been in " the Houfe he would have prevented it; " they knew that, and therefore would not " fuffer him to come amongft them." Such will be the reafoning, and fuch the confe-quences attending this meafure; but they are not the only confequences which ought to be weighed and confidered, before you engage in it. Look a little forward to the courfe of your future proceedings, and fee in what difficulties you will involve your-felves. In the prefent difpofition of the county of Middlefex, you cannot entertain a doubt, but that Mr. Wilkes will be re-elect-ed after his expulfion. You will then pro-bably think yourfelves under a neceffity of expelling him again, and he will as certain-ly be again re-elected. What fteps can the Houfe then take to put an end to a difgrace-ful conteft, in which their juftice is arraign-ed, and their authority and dignity effential-ly

ly compromifed. You cannot, by the rules
of the Houfe, refcind the vote for excluding
Mr. Wilkes, in the fame feffion in which
it has paffed, and I know but two other methods which you can purfue. They have both
been the fubject of common converfation,
and are both almoft equally exceptionable.
You may refufe to iffue a new writ, and by
that means deprive the freeholders of this
county of the right of chufing any other
reprefentative, poffibly for the whole term
of the prefent parliament. There are fome
examples of this kind in the cafe of cor-
rupt boroughs, where this Houfe has fufpended the iffuing a new writ for the
remainder of a feffion, as a punifhment upon the voters for the moft flagrant bribery;
but I cannot believe, that it will be thought
juft or advifable to inflict the fame punifhment during the term of a whole parliament, inftead of a fingle feffion, upon the
electors of a great county, for no crime,
except that of rechufing a man whom this
Houfe had cenfured and expelled. If you
do not adopt this proceeding, the other alternative will be to bring into this Houfe,
as the knight of the fhire for Middlefex, a
man chofen by a few voters only, in contra-
diction to the declared fenfe of a great majority of the freeholders on the face of the
poll, upon a fuppofition, that all the votes
of the latter are forfeited and thrown away
on account of the expulfion of Mr. Wilkes.

If

If such a proposition shall ever be brought before us, it will then be time enough to enter into a full discussion of it; at present I will only say that, I believe there is no example of such a proceeding, that if it shall appear to be new and unfounded in the law of the land, nay, if any reasonable doubt can be entertained of its legality, the attempt to forfeit the freeholders votes in this manner will be highly alarming and dangerous. Are these then the proper expedients to check and to restrain the spirit of faction and of disorder, and to bring back the minds of men to a sense of their duty? Can we seriously think they will have that salutary effect? Surely it is time to look forwards and to try other measures. A wise government knows how to enforce with temper, or to conciliate with dignity, but a weak one is odious in the former, and contemptible in the latter. How many arguments have we heard from the administration in the course of this session, for conciliating measures towards the subjects in the American colonies, upon questions where the legislative authority of Great Britain was immediately concerned? And is not the same temper, the same spirit of conciliation, at least equally necessary towards the subjects within this kingdom, or is this the only part of the King's dominions where it is not advisable to show it? Let not any gentleman think, that by conciliation I mean a blind and base compli-

ance

ance with popular opinions, contrary to our honour or juſtice; that would indeed be unworthy of us. I mean by conciliation, a cool and temperate conduct, unmixed with paſſion, or with prejudice. No man wiſhes more than I do to ſtop any exceſs on either ſide, or is more ready to reſiſt any tumultuous violence founded upon unreaſonable clamour. Such a clamour is no more than a ſudden guſt of wind which paſſes by and is forgotten; but when the public diſcontent is founded in truth and reaſon; when the ſky lowers and hangs heavy all around us, a ſtorm may then ariſe, which may tear up the conſtitution by the roots, and ſhake the palace of the King himſelf. As for me I have given my opinion, and I have choſen to do it without concert or participation. I can aſſure the Houſe, that ſome of my neareſt friends did not know the part which I ſhould take. I determined not to tell it, that I might keep myſelf unengaged and free to change it, if I thought proper, during the courſe of the debate. I do not mean by this to ſay, that I came into the Houſe without having formed an opinion; on the contrary, I had weighed and conſidered it thoroughly, and my judgment upon it is the reſult of my moſt ſerious deliberation. I know not what others may think, or who will act with me upon this occaſion. Thoſe who were once my friends may have adopted other ideas and other principles, and even

G 2   thoſe

thofe who ftill continue to be fo, may poffibly entertain different fentiments from mine
upon this fubject. That confideration muft
not prevent me from doing juftice, but God
forbid, that they fhould not exercife the
fame liberty, and follow their opinions, as
I do mine. They know that I have not
afked one of them to attend during any
part of this bufinefs, nor have I defired
their concurrence. Many of them fit a-
round me, and I appeal to them for the
truth of what i have faid. Thus far then I
have difcharged my duty, with no other
view, but to do that which appears to me
moft conformable to the ends of juftice and
of the public welfare, moft for the fafety
and honour of the king and the kingdom.
Whilft my little endeavours can contribute
but a mite to thefe great purpofes, I will
continue to exert them as freely as I have
now done ; but whenever the violence or
corruption of the times, either within or
without thefe walls, will not permit me to
follow thofe dictates uncontrouled, I will
leave this place and retire from an affembly,
which can no longer be called a free parliament. Many extravagancies committed by
Mr. Wilkes and his adherents have been urged, and even magnified, as if they could
juftify any extravagance of power to reprefs
them. It has been afked, are thefe offences
to pafs unpunifhed, and are we not to vindicate our own credit, as well as that of the
government,

government, by expreffing our abhorrence of them ? Have I been an advocate for their paffing unpunifhed ? Have I ftopped or neglected to enforce the cenfure of the law ? Was he not profecuted, tried and convicted, and when he left the kingdom to avoid his fentence, was he not outlawed ? Let me go farther. Had Mr. Wilkes ventured to return home whilft I had the honour to be entrufted with the executive powers of the ftate, he fhould not have remained out of cuftody four and twenty hours, without fubmitting himfelf to the juftice or the mercy of the King, whom he had fo grievoufly offended. He knew it, and therefore did not return till he met with more encouragement. This furely was not the behaviour, nor is this the language of one of his partizans. Compare it with the conduct of thofe who now hold the chief office and authority of the government, and who call fo loudly for vengeance and for punifhment. Did they not give their fupport to him abroad after his conviction and outlawry, and keep up an intercourfe and correfpondence with him, even whilft they were the King's minifters ? Was he not permitted to return to England, to appear publicly in this capital, for months together, and to walk daily under the windows of the palace unmolefted, unconfined, and unpunifhed ? They could not plead ignorance of the feditious libel againft

the

the King and both Houses of Parliament, nor of the three impious libels contained in the Essay upon Woman, for all of which he had been legally tried and convicted. Why then was he not called to his sentence, and the laws carried into execution, agreeable to the solemn assurances given by the King in answer to both Houses of Parliament, when they jointly addressed his majesty to carry on this prosecution? What was become of the executive power, and how were those who were invested with it justified in suspending the usual course of the law, against the express direction of the King, enforced by the recommendation of both Houses of Parliament? What were the inducements at that time to such extraordinary favour and lenity, and what are now the motives for this extraordinary resentment and severity? The first circumstance which seems to have awakened their attention, was Mr. Wilkes offering himself a candidate for the city of London and the county of Middlesex, against the inclination of the ministry: but the proceedings against him were then carried on like the feeble efforts of men not half awake, or not half in earnest. Many days passed over before the officers of the crown would venture to execute the common process of the law for apprehending him; and to obviate this difficulty, they had at last recourse to the shameful expedient of stipulating with
Mr.

Mr. Wilkes himself, the terms upon which he would confent to be taken into cuftody. To follow that precedent you ought now at leaft to afk him, upon what terms he will confent to be expelled. Perhaps, if properly applied to, he may condefcend to this requeft as gracioufly as he did to the former, and as voluntarily as he furrendered himfelf a prifoner, when he was taken with impunity out of the hands of the officers of juftice by twenty perfons, almoft in fight of the court of King's Bench then fitting in Weftminfter hall. Such was the firm and fpirited conduct by which the fupreme authority of the laws was fupported and preferved. The outlawry was reverfed for an error fo trivial, that the court of King's Bench declared when they reverfed it, that they were almoft afhamed to mention it. When the judgment was given, the firft law officer of the crown in demanding it did not think proper to enforce the penalty according to cuftom, and it was therefore milder than ufual. In the firft feffion of this parliament, Mr. Wilkes was returned a member of it, and fuffered to continue without any notice taken of him! The beginning of the prefent feffion paffed in the fame manner. What is it then which has roufed the languid fpirit of adminiftration, and called down the vengeance of the Houfe of Commons of Great Britain? Not the feditious and dangerous libel of

the

the North Briton, not the impious libels of
the Effay upon Woman, not all the extravagancies which have been urged in this
day's debate; all thefe were known before,
and were not deemed fufficient for the ex-
ertion of the common cenfures of the law;
but he has fince prefumed to write an info-
lent libel upon a fecretary of ftate. This
it feems is that capital and decifive offence,
which is to raife our indignation to its higheft pitch. The honour of our King, and
the reverence due to our Religion, were
paffed over in filence and forgotten. They
are now to be thrown into the fcale, to
make up the weight, and to induce us to
efpoufe the quarrel of a minifter. To accomplifh this important purpofe, we are to
violate not only the forms, but the effence
of our conftitution. The Houfe of Commons is to blend the executive and judicial
powers of the ftate with the legiflative, to
extend their jurifdiction, that they may take
upon themfelves the odium of trying and
punifhing in a fummary manner, an offence
which does not relate to themfelves, but is
under the immediate cognizance of the
courts of law. In the exercife of it they
are to form an accumulative and complicated charge, which no other court, nor even
they themfelves, have ever admitted in any
other inftance. They are to mingle up new
crimes with old, and to try a man twice by
the fame judicature for the fame offence.
They

They are to transfer the censures of a former parliament, contrary to all precedent, and to make them the foundation of the proceedings of a subsequent one. They are to assume a power to determine upon the rights of the people, and of their representatives, by no other rule, but that of their own inclination or discretion; and lastly, they are to attempt to persuade mankind, that they do all these things to vindicate their own honour, to express their respect for their King, and their zeal for the sacred names of their God, and their Religion. Thus are we to add hypocrisy to violence, and artifice to oppression, not remembering, that falshood and dissimulation are only the wrong sides of good sense and ability, which fools put on, and think they wear the robe of wisdom. If the House of Commons shall suffer themselves to be made the instruments, in such hands, to carry such a plan into execution, they will fall into the lowest state of humiliation and contempt. An individual indeed may exempt himself from the disgrace attending it, but the dishonour and odium of it will cleave to that Assembly, which ought to be the constant object of public reverence and affection. I have done my duty in endeavouring to prevent it, and am therefore careless of the consequences of it to myself. I expect that what I have said will be misrepresented out of

H   this

this Houfe, perhaps in that place, where of all others a mifreprefentation of what paffes here will be moft criminal. Thofe who have heard me muft know, that I have neither invidioufly aggravated, nor factioufly extenuated Mr. Wilkes's offences. If he fhall commit frefh crimes, they will call for frefh punifhment, the law is open, that law which is the fecurity of us all, to which Mr. Wilkes has been, and certainly will be amenable. Let him undergo the penalties of that law, whatever they may be, but not of an undefined, difcretionary power, the extent of which no man knows, the extent of the mifchiefs arifing from it, to every thing which is dear to us, no man can tell.

I feel that I have troubled the Houfe too long, but this is no common Queftion, and I truft, that the fame indulgence which has been my encouragement, will be my excufe and juftification.

www.ingramcontent.com/pod-product-compliance
Lightning Source LLC
Chambersburg PA
CBHW021233260626
47172CB00002B/742

* 9 7 8 3 3 3 7 1 9 5 7 4 8 *